'Self's sexually explicit fable bubbles with filth and bile, and Martin Rowson's splendid illustrations always rise to the occasion. The final descent into sexual hell is particularly memorable . . . spot-on' *Independent on Sunday*

'A caricaturistic tour de force' *Time Out*

'Self tells this story with such shrill observations towards his vacuous, loathsome characters and their surroundings that you can do nothing but dislike each and every single one of them' *Big Issue*

'Self is the master of the art of a telling sentence, and his portrait is instnatly recognisable from his swaggering prose . . . Self and Rowson take the reader into the realm of Burrough's "abysmal depths", exhibiting all the alchemic possibilities of narcotics' *Observer*

LM 1396830 0

It looks like it's going to be quite a Christmas for Richard Hermes, a Christmas powdered with cocaine, and whining with the white noise of urban derangement. Not so much enfolded, as trapped in the bosom of the nastiest, most venal media clique in London, Richard is losing it on all fronts: he's losing his heart to the nubile Ursula Bentley; he's in danger of losing his job at the pretentious listings magazine *Rendezvous*; he's losing his mind courtesy of Señor Pablo Escobar; but worst of all he's losing his soul . . . to Bell.

Bell is the king-pin, the Grand Panjandrum. He is a veritable Vautrin, guiding the ship of scandal through the lower depths. From his headquarters in Soho's Sealink Club he pulls the strings that control disseminators of drek and gatherers of glib. Bell is a newspaper columnist, a talk radio host and that incarnated oxymoron – a television personality.

But Bell has had Ursula Bentley and just about everybody else, male or female. As Richard Hermes pursues her deeper and deeper into the hinterland of debauchery, he is lured on by the sweet, seductive fragrance of her perfume, Jicki, and another, more sinister smell.

the sweet smell of
psychosis
Will Self

Illustrations by Martin Rowson

BLOOMSBURY

LONDON · BERLIN · NEW YORK · SYDNEY

First published in Great Britain 1996
This paperback edition first published 2011

Bloomsbury Publishing Plc,
50 Bedford Square, London WC1B 3DP

Text copyright © 1996 by Will Self
Illustrations copyright © 1996 by Martin Rowson

The moral right of the authors has been asserted

A CIP catalogue record for this book
is available from the British Library

ISBN 978 1 408 82739 0

10 9 8 7 6 5 4

Typeset by Hewer Text Ltd, Edinburgh
Printed by Clays Ltd, St Ives plc.

For Victoria and Anna

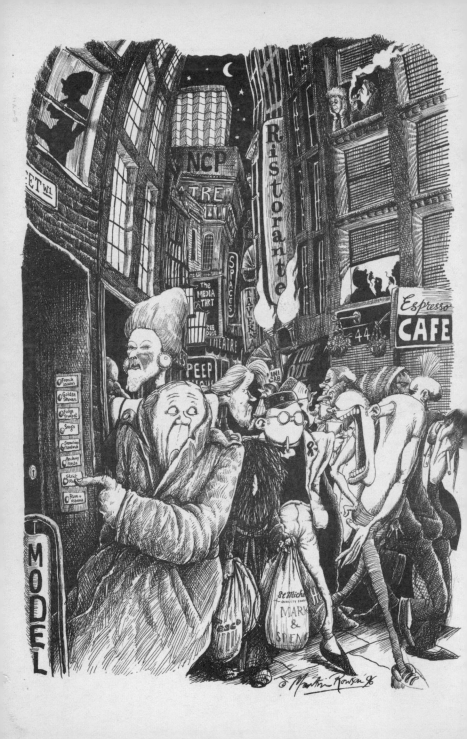

Two men stood by a window in one of the private rooms of the Sealink Club, and watched a third who was hovering around on the corner of D'Arblay Street. The man they were watching was plump, in his late thirties and wearing a mid-price trench coat. His thin, brown hair wasn't making it all the way over his pate. The two watchers could see this distinctly, because they were four flights up and looking more or less straight down.

'I don't think he's going to do it,' said Richard Hermes. 'I think he's going to go home to wifey.'

'I'm not so sure,' replied his companion, Todd Reiser, taking a pull on the joint they were sharing. 'He almost definitely wants to – it's just a question of getting his bottle together.'

The man on the corner moved to the edge of the kerb, as if about to cross the road and head off, but then turned once more to look at the building behind him.

It was a nondescript place, made timeless by grime, the portico studded with bellpushes. Even though Richard couldn't make them out at this range, he knew that above the bellpushes were Sellotaped bits of paper or card with 'MODEL' written on them. There was also a freestanding sign to one side of the doorway, like the ones that rotate in the slipstream by roadside petrol stations, displaying first the legend 'PETROL' and then the legend 'DERV'. But this sign simply stated 'MODEL', and when it revolved reiterated it.

The trench-coated potential punter was havering once more, rocking from heels to toes on the very edge of the pavement. 'Five quid says he'll do it,' Todd said, pulling a crumpled note from the side pocket of his jacket.

'All right, you're on.' Richard didn't want the man on the corner to go up and fuck one of the brasses. Richard wanted him to walk down to Tottenham Court Road and take the Central Line back to Parsons Green, or Turnham Green, or whichever Green it was he lived at, and stroll back from the station to wifey, with his conscience clear and his cock unscented with spermicidal lubricant. Richard wanted this quite passionately.

Suddenly, as if the man were actually responding to the thoughts of the two voyeurs, he turned on the spot, glanced quickly up and down the street, and bolted into the building. Richard and Todd continued to watch as his – now distinctive – profile appeared first at the window of the first-floor landing, then at the window of the second, then the third.

'Must be viewing the merchandise on the up escalator,' Todd sneered.

'Or perhaps he knows where he's going,' Richard replied.

Then they couldn't see him any more. Richard sighed, trying to picture what was going on in there. The uneven floor of the brass's room, thinly, dunly carpeted. The bed – what could that possibly be like? A vessel built for a thousand short transports, none of them delightful. A roll-on, roll-off kind of bed, collapsed and pummelled. Richard imagined the odour of the place, compounded of the cheapest of perfumes, cigarette smoke, legions of cocks, more legions of condoms. Over it all the almost faecal odour of baby oil. And what of the brass herself? Some grimacing ugly, Richard decided, coldly presenting her dry gash to the balding man as he took off his trench coat, folded it, placed it on a three-legged chair.

'Where's that fiver then?' Todd interrupted his thoughts, stamped on them with his leather-sole tongue. Then he passed Richard the joint, which was by now little more than a stub. Richard faffed around trying to avoid burning himself while he forced his hand into the tight pocket of his jeans.

But the trench-coated man had reappeared. He came out of the front door of the knocking shop at a brisk trot.

'Look at him!' Todd expostulated. 'He's got the wind up him now.'

Richard ceased looking for the fiver. 'You've lost,' he said.

'Whassat?'

'You've lost,' Richard said again. 'I mean to say, no one could have fucked anybody in the time he was up there.'

'Huh. S'pose. Well, here you are then.' Todd pulled a different, rolled-up fiver from his pocket and handed it to Richard, who noticed with minor revulsion an encrustation of dried snot and blood at one end. 'Home to wifey it is − I hope he doesn't have any regrets.' He departed, slamming the door behind him.

However, as Richard continued to watch, the man didn't head for home. Far from it. He crossed the road diagonally and disappeared below the horizon of the windowsill. He was – Richard realised with a jolt – coming into the Sealink. Richard was surprised, if not exactly astounded. Chances were, if the man was a member of the Sealink, that he had something to do with the media, and was vulnerable if recognised. Perhaps he didn't care? Perhaps there was no wifey, back at the Green, taking the casserole off the hob, leaving it to settle, leaving it to cool.

Richard sighed. He was a young man, slim, of medium height, with curly, blond hair. His features had something strained and delicate about them; blue veins showed at eyelid and ear curl. His expression was usually purposive, quizzical, lacking – as yet – urban guile. There was no wifey at home for Richard. No girlfriend either. Not so much, he grimly meditated, as a dry-gashed brass.

The words felt ugly enough in his mind to produce a bitter sensation on his tongue. Richard wasn't really that crude a young man. He half-hawked, swallowed his own bile, hunched his shoulders, shivered, and then followed in Todd Reiser's wake, out of the door, down the orange-carpeted, winding stairs, and into the bar.

It was late on in the cocktail period and the atmosphere in the Sealink Club bar was, to say the least, rocky. Over the past couple of hours a lot of rebarbative, ulcerated and embittered people had been working hard at bedding their resentments down in sensory-deprivation tanks full of alcohol. In this no-alternative therapy, they were ably assisted by Julius, the club's chief barman. He pirouetted up and down behind the big, mirrored buckler of the bar, waltzing bottles of whisky, gin and vodka from shelf to glass. He did the cancan with the shaker, the lambada with the ice cubes, the Charleston with the bottled beers. He was a snappy mover. His bright orange hair was sculpted into a Cubist divot, his earrings were jade studs, his shirt, apron and bow tie were immaculate, gleaming. His deportment was so irrefutably *classy* that – as is often the case – the members of this exclusive club looked shabby by association.

Richard took this all in from the small lobby area outside the bar, before entering. To do so he had to near-clamber over the raised sill of the door. It was these sills, together with the functionalist decor of the establishment – naked bulbs behind wire basketry, bright orange floorcoverings, steel furniture bolted to those floors – and the persistent humming judder which perfused the place, that had gifted it its name. For the club was sited in a building directly above the main terminus of the Post Office's miniature underground railway, and the committee had elected to make a thematic virtue out of an urban necessity. But more importantly, to be in the Sealink *was* to be at sea – in more senses than one.

Then the human hubbub assailed Richard. Advertising people, television people, media-associated subsidiary professionals, jingle music composers, voiceover actors, public relations people, design consultants, gallery girls, commercial artists and a fair littering of moneyed or titled deadbeats. These were the denizens of the Sealink. They all seemed to smoke, they all seemed to drink, they all held themselves in exaggerated postures, heads jerking around, on the lookout for better social prospects lying behind the heads – or the bodies – of their interlocutors.

So pervasive in the bar of the Sealink was this tendency to scan all parts of the room, other than the faces of

your immediate neighbours, that it resulted in a kind of collective perturbation, like an agitated, atomised Mexican wave. Richard absorbed this wriggle of regard, felt it wash over him. He too began to scan, check out who was there, who he knew, who was interesting, who had something to offer.

Richard didn't have to suffer this motor pattern for long, though, because over in his usual corner was Bell, and with him was the divine, the untouchable, the universally desirable Ursula Bentley. Richard's pulse quickened – the semi-bald John was forgotten in that instant. Todd Reiser was with them as well, as were a number of other clique members. Bell's limpid black eyes met Richard's from some thirty feet away, Bell's Martini glass forming a tiny, vitreous horizon. Bell raised one finger and tapped it against the dead centre of his forehead. This was a kind of trademarked gesture of Bell's – one of them, at any rate. It meant 'You may ring my bell . . .', or, more to the point, 'I will deign to speak to you'. Richard hurried over.

There is, of course, one significant group of club members that has been omitted from the list above. A group that Richard, insignificantly, belonged to. These were the hacks, for, if the Sealink Club had one prime *raison d'être*, it was the provision of a dark, humid environment in which fungal tittle-tattle could swell overnight. This was the damp cellar of the city.

There was a ratio of hacks to non-hacks in the bar at this time of about one to one. And these weren't principled journalists, or hardened reporters, oh no. No one eased his leaning position at the bar in order to relieve the pressure on the shrapnel wound he'd caught covering the Balkan crisis. Nor did anyone huddle in a corner earnestly discussing *her* view of the Neo-Keynesian implications of the Treasury's management of the Public Sector Borrowing Requirement. Not a bit of it.

The hacks who frequented the Sealink, yakking in the bar, gobbling in the restaurant, goggling in the television room, wobbling in the table-football room, and snorting in the toilets, occupied a quite different position in the cultural food chain. They were transmitters of trivia, broadcasters of banality, and disseminators of drek. They wrote articles about articles, made television programmes about television programmes, and commented on what others had said. They trafficked in the glibbest, slightest, most ephemeral cultural reflexivity, enacting a dialogue between society and its conscience that had all the resonance of a foil individual pie dish smitten with a paperclip.

Along with so many others around the bar, gathered in their crap colloquia, Richard laboured by day in this open-cast word mine, hauling out great truckles of frothy verbiage. Nominally responsible for a front-of-house, arts/cultural, gossip-cum-preview section in a mass-circulation listings magazine, Richard also filed featureless features for some of the men's glossy style magazines, extolling the virtues of trouser presses, aromatherapy and ski-boarding.

He was uncertain about this role in life – it was so new to him. A year previously he had been on the news desk of a homely, old newspaper, in a homely, old, northern city. He had had a girlfriend tending towards parturition, and a small flat that would have required partition.

Then a couple of features he had written on spec for London magazines found a home, and the praise had gone to his feet, which strode to the managing editor's desk, to his mouth, which mouthed his resignation, and to his cock, which shrank from the homely, muslin confines of his girlfriend's vagina. Richard headed south – geographically.

In London he landed the job, and rented a flatlet in Hornsey. A grim little box, made all the grimmer by its pretension to being a real dwelling place. Everything about it was diminutive – the bed, the chairs, the cooker. Even the lintels of the doors were at least six inches lower than they really ought to be, which meant that whenever Richard came home late, or drunk, or both (which was more often than not the case), he found himself headbutting the architrave as he moved from roomlet to roomlet.

While his living space was still more diminished down south, his social horizons were confused. He was amazed at how well he got on in town; he had expected the going to be sticky, fraught with snobbery and bitchery. But his fellow hacks fell on him as if he were some entirely novel creature, a positive Ariel charming their isle of tedium. The fact that he had worked in the North, that he had been to a minor public school, that he spoke unaffectedly of home and parents – these were regarded as quirky and compelling characteristics, landing him invitations to party, after party, after party, where Bulgarian wines were poured down the neck from the neck, in the bottlenecks by the makeshift bars.

After these gigs – openings, or launches, or press beanos – Richard would carry on in the train of the revellers. They would process to the West End clubs, and those in their number who had membership would shoehorn them in, to Soho House, or Fred's, or the Groucho, or, of course, the Sealink – that premier preening place, that atelier of arrogance.

Richard was impressed by the Sealink. He saw movie stars there, pop musicians and, most importantly, the stars of his own profession – the superhacks. High-maintenance girls sashayed across the orange floorcoverings, and Richard goggled at them, lusted after them. He'd had no sex of any kind in the past year, save for two frenzied couplings with his immediate boss at the magazine, a successful anorexic in her forties who turned out to be a glove fetishist. He had balked at a third coupling, when she'd asked him to don oven gloves before scratching her pork. Needless to say this hadn't – as he had feared – affected their working relationship. She ignored him as effectively as she had done before.

But the girls in the Sealink! AAAAOOOOOOOH! How he lusted after them! Their glossy hair and cigarette skin! Their whining voices and wasted eyes!

Their air of thoroughgoing contempt − expensively studied disregard. They glided about the place, and Richard followed the cruxes of their bodies, his eyes flickering, precisely registering each tilt and cant they made, while he visualised the subtle accommodations of their clothing, their hair, their skin . . .

Foremost among these glibmaidens, calling from the trivial rocks, was Ursula Bentley. Ursula wrote a diary for a glossy monthly detailing her amorous adventures. It was the most embarrassingly awful column Richard had ever read, but he made enormous allowances for her, allowances the size of Third World debts. He wanted her. She was not simply beautiful, but beautiful in a way that was so vastly improbable − like a diamond found in a gutter behind a Chinese takeaway − that to Richard, silly fool, she redeemed him, her, all of the sordidity and sopor, the tragic bathos that he felt sloshing about the Sealink.

That was how Bell snagged him in, made Richard part of his little group.

Richard took his allotted seat and signed for one of the waiters, knowing full well that given his lowly status he might wait some tens of minutes for a drink. Bell was − as usual − silent. He was sitting in the bosom of his clique like a big-bodied spider in the middle of its web; invisible filaments wreathed him, garbed him, filaments of gossip and speculation, of opinion and dissent. And Bell sat there, listening to it all, registering it all, masticating it all for future regurgitation.

For if the Sealink Club had a kingpin, a grand panjandrum, a veritable Vautrin guiding the ship of scandal from the lower depths, then it was Bell. Bell was a hack, true enough, but he was also much more than that. His daily syndicated column ran in both the *Standard* and the *Mail*, reaching some ten million ideologically hobbled readers. His weekly television programme – a chat show called *Campanology* – was broadcast at peak viewing time on Friday night, live to some fifteen million viewers. His dead-zone phone-in show on Talk Radio may have gone out between two and four a.m. on a Sunday morning (although recorded six hours previously), but it none the less managed to buzz in the ears of some four hundred thousand lost souls.

Given the Venn intersections implied by this saturation coverage, one of Bell's most sycophantic acolytes had established – through certain arcane statistical computations – that there must, logically, be at least two hundred thousand people in Britain who did *nothing else* but listen to Bell's voice, watch Bell's face, or read his words, for every waking hour of their lives. The same sycophant had once earned a week of his mentor's approval by seriously floating the idea that Bell should act now to broadcast to the subconscious and thus colonise the dreamscape.

Bell was a heavily-built man in his late thirties. He was thick both straight through and transversely. This would have made him curiously blocky and four-square, had it not been for the fact that his façade was so flat, so two-dimensional, as to cheat the eye. Hardly anyone ever looked at Bell and thought in terms of his mass, his solidity; rather, it was the front that bewitched the eye. Given his reputation, no one could have expected it when seeing him *in the flesh*, but Bell was good-looking, neat, nicely clean in appearance. His torso was one rectangle, his arms two thinner ones. His legs were congruent with his arms. He wore plain, well-cut suits that emphasised these planes.

This was just as well. More perspicacious, trained observers who managed to stay athwart Bell – in, as it were, a potential boarding position – for long enough could gain some sense of his true heft. Beneath the finely woven wool was a body of awesome strength. A minotaur body, half–bull, half–man, thick of bone and intractable of muscle. Bell even held himself as the Minotaur might have done: bent forward from the waist, legs braced against the deck of the Sealink, arms pushed out and forward, so as to occupy the most propitious pyramid of space, so as to make good any lack of *gravitas* with a perfect centre of gravity.

Then there was the head. Once more, all the angles were well exploited by the man. Hardly anyone really knew that Bell was more or less neckless, that a lithic tier of fat 'n' muscle made a pagoda of his upper storey. Hardly anyone – not even those who had slept with Bell, who had had those jutting jaws clamped on their remote (or proximate) sensors – had noticed the prognathous, not to say primitive, cast of that face. Rather, encountering it from the public, the front-of-house angle, they often found him . . . surprisingly pretty.

Glossy black hair hung in loose bangs around a high, white forehead. The eyes were black – but warmly so. The flawless complexion was pointed up by a small, bell–shaped birthmark on the edge of his jaw.

The lips were red – but not wet. The nose, though broad-bridged, had fine nostrils. And there was more than enough bone in cheek and chin to supply the suffix. No wonder that Bell scored – and scored often. Scored, more or less, whenever and with whomever he wanted.

Even in a rout of rutting like the Sealink, Bell's penchant for cunt and cock stood out. He liked them both. Some bar dross said the former more, others the latter. Whatever the case, Bell had no difficulties in obtaining supplies. Of course, in his line of work there were the facile, the futile, and the febrile seductions: those loose enough, insubstantial enough, and weak enough for their heels to round under the man's hooded gaze, to find themselves tipping over backwards, knees and thighs arranged automatically into the correct position for effective penetration.

But Bell didn't simply forage on the herbage within reach of his big mouth, oh no. He was also capable of seducing those who attempted to evade him, to outrun the silvered tongue, trajected like bolas to wrap around their lower limbs, pull them down to the plushly carpeted pampa. There were many of these, for – damn it all! – even the denizens of the West End have some pride, some integrity, some other relationship they don't wish to lose.

These Bell particularly favoured with his attentions. It seemed a perfect tonic to the man to seek out some long-established relationship – marriage, cohabitation, or a clandestine affair, even – and interpose his dissolutive bulk between the pair-bonding, unsticking the accretions of years, experiences, children . . . even love.

Innumerable weeping spouses, girlfriends, boy-friends, partners and lovers had raged impotently up and down the stretch of unforgiving pavement outside Bell's mansion-house block in Bloomsbury. Bell never made any attempt to hide his peccadilloes. In fact, that his corporeal column should have as much salience as his printed one seemed to be at the core of his philandering. And he always got his man, or his woman. So much so that once the denizens of the Sealink were aware even that he had drawn a bead on a given target, they knew that it was only a matter of time before there would be tears in the toilets, sobbing on the lobby phone, altercations in the vestibule. Laclos would have had a field day with Bell.

It was one such annihilation of affect that the clique were discussing as Richard tuned in, adjusting his ears to the whine of perfidy. Ursula Bentley was saying, 'Really, I think she'll have to go somewhere, a clinic . . . whatever, cool off, y'know what I mean – '

'But I don't think it's exactly drugs that're the problem.' This was from a man called Slatter, who ran a clippings service much patronised by Bell.

'Hng'f – ' Ursula snorted, her lovely mouth distorted with contempt, 'if it's not drugs, it bloody well *ought* to be. Bell says she was banging on the main door of his block at five in the morning, twitching, white-faced, the whole bit. Isn't that right, Bell?' She turned her radiant eyes to her mentor, who inclined his massive head ever so slightly to indicate that this was indeed the case.

Slatter had been shaping a rejoinder, some of his words even ran under the end of Ursula's explanation, but seeing Bell's acquiescence he immediately shut up and fell to examining his nails. He was a beatifically repugnant man, Slatter. Thin and yet sallowly saggy, he always wore off-the-peg suits that appeared cut from fabric with the texture of vinyl (in summer), or carpet underlay (in winter). There were mounds of 'druff on his shoulders, and scurf clearly visible on his scalp. The nails he was examining were so neatly encrusted – each with a dear little dark crescent – that the crud essence was almost decorative. But in spite – or, perhaps, more sinisterly, *because* – of this, Slatter was Bell's right-hand man, his factotum, his chore whore. It was he who ran errands, took messages, bought cocaine, sold weepy girls down the river to abortionists in Edgware.

His dirty hands guaranteed Bell's clean ones. And as befits a parasite and host who have achieved a perfect *modus vivendi*, they were in symbiosis, oblivious of who occupied which role.

Bell was still silent; the filaments of unease and control connecting him to the other clique members hummed and pulsed. Who, Richard wondered, would seize this opportunity to advance himself, to take on the responsibility of providing input, material, potential copy?

It was Todd Reiser. 'You'll never guess,' he began, 'what young Richard and I saw just now . . .' Reiser's collar-length, glossy hair bounced on the collar of his hacking jacket as he leant forward, claiming the web site.

'You're right,' whined Adam Kelburn, the Deputy Editor of *Cojones*, a men's style magazine Richard wrote features for, and a distal – if enthusiastic – cliquer, 'we won't. Why not tell us, Todd?'

Reiser hunched himself up still further, to form a veritable basis of denim and whipcord, all supporting a Martini glass. 'We were up in the top room, herherh, and young Richard spotted this character hanging around outside the knocking shop opposite, h'herherher . . .' Reiser was a once-and-future film director who – naturally enough – made adverts. With everyone he was brusque to the point of rank rudeness – everyone but Bell, that was. '. . . So, we thought we'd get a little bet on, as to whether he'd actually go in and poke one of the brasses, herherh'her . . .' He paused to take a slurp of his drink, and Bell's inky tones stained the atmosphere.

'How much was the bet?' As ever, Richard was shocked by the measured evenness of the man's voice.

'The bet!' Reiser started. 'The bet, well, er . . . a fiver, wasn't it Richard?'

'That's right.'

'Anyways, this prannet goes in, trudges all the way up three flights of pokertunity. So I'm thinking I'm quids in – because that's the way I'd figured it – when he turns tail and comes barrelling all the way back down again, h'herherher . . .'

Even Reiser's sniggering exploited women, Richard thought — but then, irresistibly, the opportunity to exploit them himself began to hold sway. 'Actually,' Richard dropped into the short-term maw that had opened up to receive this anecdote, 'he didn't head for home.'

'Oh no?' Reiser crammed as much snot as he could into the two nasal vowels.

'No, he came into the club.'

'In here? Into the Sealink?' This was from Ursula. She was talking to Richard — sort of. His heart sang.

'Yeah, in fact, he's standing right over there, gabbing to Julius.'

Six pairs of calculating eyes dipped, panned, and unobtrusively zoomed, so as to get a view of this John, this consummate mark. 'H'herherh'her,' Reiser tittered, 'well I'll be buggered, young Richard's right!'

Everyone ignored him, because by certain subtle, even obscure, movements, Bell was indicating that he wished to speak. 'OK,' he pronounced, 'let's have a little fun. Slatter, go to the front desk and find out bald boy's name. Reiser, you go with him. Once you've got hold of the handle, you go across the road. You say he went up to the top floor, well, it's obviously the whore up there who he either wanted to see, or couldn't bear the sight of. Give her some dosh, and get her to come back across here, sign herself in as baldy's guest, come into the bar and *faire un petit rendezvous*. That should stop us all from expiring with boredom, huh?'

Richard was stunned with a vibrating, cacophonous silence. He felt as if someone had clubbed him round the head with a two-pound fillet of wet fish.

He was still stunned three hours later, sitting on a stool in the farthest corner of The Hole, an illegal drinking club in a sub-sub-basement beneath a porn 'n' poppers shop on Old Compton Street. Richard was stunned by the sheer, wilful malice of it. He could still remember the expression on the poor man's face when the whore had come into the bar, sidled up to him, put her bruised arm through the epaulette of his trench coat, nuzzled her peroxided brow into his shoulder. Richard remembered the man's face, myopic, hurting, as the red had suffused from his neck, up through the sparse roots of his sparse hair. And Richard felt the shame he had provoked.

Now, he sat morosely, hanging on to a small plank of sobriety, while all around was a choppy sea of inebriation. Bell was there as well. He was standing

now, standing and chatting, completely at ease, with two huge black guys dressed in string vests and dungarees. Bell was in his element, adjusting his posture to match theirs, and – Richard could just make this out above the background roar – adopting some of their tags, their Whadjas, Safes and Seens, to customise his patter, make him accessible to his listeners.

Ursula was there too. She was still pristine, even at this late hour. Richard could see no reddening of her blue eyes, or lankening of her thick, chestnut swathe of hair. Rather, the long evening of drinking seemed to have given her still more life, more embodiment. He hid behind his drunkenness as if it were a tree, and peered out at her. How could she hang around with these people? How could she witness cruel jokes like the one they'd played on the trench-coated man, without somehow becoming corrupted in her very essence? How could she?

Richard realised he was in danger of making a fool of himself. He was too drunk for this. When he weaved across the crowded basement, to take his place in the terminal toilet stall to gush and drain, he banged ankles, nudged paper cups. The imprecations floated into his ears as if from a long way off, shouted across a vale of tears. I'm staying up, he deliberated deliberately as he focused on the precise point at which piss exited from penis, so that she won't go home with him. Will she go home with him? Oh! Will she?!

Of course, Richard knew that she had in the past. There were hardly any of the permanent crew around Bell who hadn't. But it was merely his way of branding them with his mark, a badge of admission. Once he'd done it, he didn't do it again . . . or did he? She was so – so *fucking desirable*. Perfect figure: large, pointed breasts, requiring no girding or uplift; waist cinched for holding; swivel hips and long, lolloping legs; and that face! The eyes permanently, violet-violently astonished; the brows straight slashes of brown; the whole rounded and yet sharp, with skin of an absolute pink flawlessness stretched over it. Ursula had told Richard – apropos of nothing – that she never wore makeup; that her toilet consisted only of a little moisturiser, and Jicki, the subtle, irrepressibly erotic fragrance created by Guerlain for the Empress Eugénie.

A little moisturiser! Richard wanted to be the little moisturiser. Wanted to be dabbed by a cotton-wool pad against those cheeks, that neck, those breasts. Oh Jesus! She wouldn't cross the road to piss on him, he was certain of that. But he couldn't leave her here. He couldn't . . .

'. . . Still hanging in, are we, young Richard?' said Todd Reiser, looming over him. Reiser could do this because Richard was slumped down on the stool. The director was a nice example of praxis: he was short, and he also shot shorts. He also wore irritating jeans, which should have been but weren't creased. He affected shirts of heavy texture as well, and Richard couldn't forbear from imagining still grimmer top garments in the recesses of the Reiser wardrobe – zip-up cardigans, and sleeveless Fair Isle sweaters. 'You know, I don't think you stand much of a chance in that direction . . .' Reiser smirked – so it seemed to Richard – his entire body towards the lovely Ms Bentley.

A small compartment full of bile opened up in the back of Richard's throat. 'W'f, w'reurgh,' he expostulated, then found himself up on his hind legs, tottering like a foal soused with Campari, and also – equally involuntarily – muttering 'G'night' in Bell's, Ursula's and Reiser's general direction. Then he was in Old Compton Street haggling prices with the tribally scarred, clipboard-bearing cab controller, outside the kiosk by the Pollo Bar.

Soon afterwards the cab was heading north, up Tottenham Court Road. Richard slopped around in the back seat, mostly anaesthetised, yet at one and the same time fully alert to the shock of tyre over pothole.

At the junction with the Euston Road a huge hoarding was positioned so as to obscure a building site abutting the Euston Tower. Richard bleared at the thing, seeing dawn flush above its top edge – and then took it in more fully. It was one of those three-in-one hoardings, a rack of rotating triangular bars; and as the cab idled by the lights, a woman's pudenda encased in a flawless, silken second skin started to riffle like a pack of cards being spread for the cut, and gave way to those familiar features, the red lips, the broad-bridged nose. Bell's warm, black eyes looked out at Richard; Bell's big digit tapped Bell's high, white forehead. The advert's slogan was the last thing that the hoarding made legible, flipped over into comprehension: 'All Through the Night on MW 1053/1089 kHz. Get Hold of That Clapper – and Ring Me, Bell.'

The traffic lights clicked, the parted legs of the green iconic man married, the cabbie engaged drive, the car lurched forward, Richard's head fell back against the seat. Where were those red lips now? Perhaps nuzzling

the silken skin that encased Ursula? Richard groaned throatily; the cabbie scrunged round in the mock-leather confines of his car coat. 'What yer doin'?' he demanded, sensing with professional acumen the vomit and bile that were welling in Richard's throat.

'No – gr'nff – no really, 's all right.'

They drove on. Never had Hornsey seemed so much of a haven to Richard.

The following morning Richard was sitting in the editorial meeting at *Rendezvous*, the loathsome and affected listings magazine he worked for, when one of the subs came in with a Post-it note fluttering on her fingertip. She walked round to where Richard was sitting – next to his superior, the glove fetishist – and transferred the adhesive notelet from her finger to his. Richard squinted down at the scrap of information. It read: 'Ursula Bentley rang. Please call her on 602 3368. *Urgent!*'

Richard hadn't been thinking about Chico Fran-quini's new film *Grave Robber*, nor had he been giving much attention to the forthcoming Shell Oil Festival of Indigenous Music; the Kandinsky show at the Bankside did not impinge, and neither did Company Corneille's staging at Sadler's Wells of the original Diaghilev *Rite of Spring*. On the muddy, polluted foreshore of Richard's consciousness, the cultural waves slapped limply; towards the horizon a ruptured tanker wallowed in the curdling sea. Richard had grasped the magnitude of the disaster at dawn, in bed in Hornsey, when he saw the thick slick of wine, beer and vodka gushing from the tanker's hull, and the dark pall of dope smoke overhead.

It was going to be a day of getting through things – endeavouring to persevere. This was not a day when Richard was going to take a fearless moral inventory and remedy his ethical deficiencies. He could just about see his way to feeling the shape of the ulcers his teeth had worried into being on the insides of his cheeks; he would do his best to disregard the phantom fat fingers that encapsulated his own; towards lunch he might counsel the atrocity exhibition of a bowel movement.

The *Rendezvous* office was hell on hangovers. Under the unphotogenic glare of strip lighting, a more than averagely nasty open plan – floor and ceiling tiling clashing and gnashing together, mashing the intervening space – was networked with thorax-high, freestanding bafflers of some composite material, covered in fabric with a rough, oatmealy nap. The journalists, subs, production people, secretaries, designers and gofers who tenanted this stunted maze moved about the place at some speed, fetching and carrying bits of paper; or else bobbed up above the partitions, to shout to some colleague that copy was coming – along the cable tracking.

Gathering by the water-cooler, on the landing outside the toilets, or on the fire stairs, the staff of *Rendezvous* smoked Silk Cut, and took tiny options on the future preoccupations of the mass of their fellow Londoners. They earnestly debated the opening of themed restaurants, and the demise of experimental opera productions, as if they were matters of millennial import that would define an era. Even on a good day it made Richard feel nauseous.

The apex of this pyramid of ephemera, ministered to by a pretentious priesthood, was the morning editorial meeting. As a deputy section editor, Richard attended this two days a week. These were the meetings at which things actually got done – when it was the section heads alone, they merely intrigued. But after all, Richard thought, what did his work consist of? Reducing some forthcoming event still further than it reduced itself? Producing a kind of stock of the culture? He would write a hundred and fifty words, on a novel, a play, an album, append to it a photograph the size of a postage stamp, and often – in his unhumble opinion – he would have dealt with the subject matter, the themes, better than the original.

This morning's meeting was more than averagely awful. The Editor, whose patter was compounded in equal parts of managementspeak and manipulation, was making it his business to humiliate the editor of the performance section, an unstable man with a burgeoning heroin habit. There would be tears before elevenses, Richard was thinking grimly, when the note arrived.

Her note. It smashed through the partitions – her note; and it crashed through the glass walls of the Editor's office (he'd had them installed after seeing *All the President's Men*). It ushered in a coconut-scented breeze, the sound of a Hawaiian guitar. The thick slick of alcohol began to be cleaned up with the detergent of desire. The dark pall of dope smoke wavered and dispersed. His eyes still clamped on the Post-it note, Richard saw the future opening up before him like some virgin land. It was a future in which Ursula Bentley called him at the office. It was nirvana.

Richard made it through the rest of the meeting by grinding the shaft of his erect penis against the underside edge of the conference table until a sharp pain ran down his inner thigh. Once or twice he thought that this extraordinary practice might actually cause him to ejaculate, but he had to do it, had to prevent himself from being carried away on a cloud of mucal imaginings. Richard didn't even rise when the glove fetishist – in a lull – flicked his golden calf of a Post-it note with a fake nail and insinuated, 'Well, Richard, Ursula Bentley eh? Pretty thing, isn't she – although, to coin a phrase, she's had *her* bell rung a fair few times, hmm?'

As soon as the meeting ended, Richard sprinted through the maze of partitioning like an experimental rat hurrying to get an on-demand hit of cocaine. He crouched down in the cul-de-sac that served him as an office space, and dialled the number on the note. It was a Kensington exchange. As the mist of static was cleared by connection, Richard's imagination called up a vision of Ursula in her Kensington flat, with its high, high ceilings, its quarter-acre of Persian rug, its cabinets full of rare *objets d'art*. There she was, Ursula, a Maughamesque figure, reclining on a deco divan in a bay window. Her gown was long, falling in columns and scallops of ivory material. There was gold at her breast, worked into her girdle, and at hem and sleeve as well. Her telephone receiver was sculpted in the form of an epicene young man, an Adonis – like Ursula herself, formed of ivory and gold.

'Yeah?' Ursula's voice rasped.

'Is – is that Ursula? Ursula B–Bentley?' Richard didn't so much reply, as warble.

'Yeah.'

'It's Richard, Richard Hermes.'

'Oh, yeah, young Richard. You scarpered a bit quick last night. What happened?' Her voice was harsh – but not to his ear.

'Um, well, work in the morning y'know – ' Fool! He didn't know that she knew anything of the sort. Apart from her column ('Peccadillo', which some wags referred to as 'Pick-a-Dildo'), Richard had no idea of what Ursula did. But judging by the way in which she waved aside everything that pertained to money – like her share of the bill – the world of work was something she orbited, rather than inhabited.

'At *Rendezvous*, with what's her name, that glove woman.'

'Sorry?' He was sorry all right, sorry that anything should connect these two. He felt as if (and this was an overarching absurdity) he had betrayed Ursula already, committed proleptic adultery.

'You know, Richard, your boss, Fabia, the glove woman. Don't tell me she hasn't tried it on with you. She got me in the coat room at some party once. I was a bit pissed, so we sort of started snogging, whatever. Then she pulled some ski gloves out of her pocket, the thick, quilted kind. Tried to get me to give her a right good frigging with them. Since then I've heard all sorts about her – but always with the glove angle. What was it with you? Leather driving numbers with holes? Mittens?'

'Oven gloves, actually.'

'Ha-ha! Very good, Richard. "*Touché*," one might even say.'

By God! He'd said something right! A thousand thousand pink flamingos lifted off from the volcanic lake of Richard's stomach.

'Well, I'm afraid *I* had nothing much to get up for this morning, so I went on with the boys.'

'W-where?' The flamingos were machine-gunned by Nazi vivisectionists.

'To that gay place by Charing Cross, then back to

The Hole again – Bell wanted to pick something up – then back to Bloomsbury.'

'T–to Bell's?'

'Yah. Then we had a gas. Bell had some of this shit called bliss. Sort of cross between smack, E and ice. You've gotta smoke it in a little pipe. Makes you feel . . . I dunno . . . Well! Like you'd imagine.

'Anyway,' Ursula went on, 'Reiser had skulked off by this time, do Bell calls him up – he knows Reiser can't resist drugs – and says, "Hey Todd, wanna come back to my place and do some bliss? The whole gang's here, plus some babes who've blown in from out of town, and want to meet people in film . . ." Todd is salivating so much *I* can hear it, going "Yeah-yeah, yeah-yeah" like fucking Muttley. So Bell just says, "Well you can't!" and slams the phone down. Ha-ha-ha-ha!'

'Hee-hee, hee-hee,' Richard joined in, although he couldn't for the life of him have said what was funny about it.

'The poor sap even came over and leant on the entryphone for half an hour before Bell got round to disconnecting it – '

'When did you get home?' Richard almost snapped this; like most courage, it was reflex.

'What?'

'I mean – back?'

'Dunno. Whatever. Six-thirty, seven. Whatever. Tweety time, at any rate – I'm fucked. Anyway, Richard, it's Mearns's greenmail party this evening, and I'm doing the APB. See you at the Club at seven – *I'll* be early . . .'

'O –'

Rrrrrrrrrrrrrrrrrrrrrrrrrrrrrrr . . .

Richard listened to the dialling tone for some time, hearing it as the Little Bear's purring, lustful breath. That's what his lovey-dovey nickname for her would be: 'Little Bear'.

Then he shook himself out of it and turned to the computer. The screen showed the corporate screensaver, a cartoon representation of an average *Rendezvous* reader (back view), ringing with a felt tip his/her cultural-event selections for the week. Richard slapped the mouse; the screen squeaked and cleared to reveal about two hundred words of copy. With a myriad flocks of pink flamingos spiralling like galaxies in his universal heart, Richard Hermes bent to the task of correcting the copy. He had been called by Ursula Bentley! They had made . . . a rendezvous! (What else could that 'early' have meant?) On such a day, even annotating pre-puff for Razza Rob's new stand-up show *Gynae-Gynae, Hey-Hey!* was a rare treat.

Richard hovered about on a metaphorical decision-making corner all day, much like the John on his actual corner the night before. At five he started for Hornsey, only to abandon the journey halfway there, leaving the tube at Archway on the grounds that he wasn't going to have enough time to get home, shower, masturbate himself into a genderless nullity (this was an evening when Richard didn't even wish for the race memory of an involuntary erection), then address the question of his toilet and attire with a rigour not seen since pubescent, preening pre-disco nightmares.

To have insufficient time at the Wendy flat would be worse than having none at all. Better to turn up at the Sealink with a devil-may-care, rumpled-from-the-night-before, funky-dirty-stopover, essentially rugged and masculine demeanour. In this macho attitude Richard would rub his stubble vigorously against Ursula's cheek upon meeting, challenging her with insolent eyes to imagine its abrasiveness applied else-where – sanding her into submission.

Richard's sagging, spotted trousers, bagging shirt

and scuffed shoes would be taken by Ursula as telling evidence of a disconcertingly sexy and powerful lack of self-consciousness. He considered whether a nice further touch might be to give a mock-Yiddisher hunch of his shoulders and declaim to her, 'Style, schmyle!'

All of this kaleidoscoped through Richard's mind as he paced up and down the tatty concourse outside Archway Tower, his eyes stinging from the grit that cold, dry puffs of wind were kicking up. At least his hangover was on the wane; all he felt now were a certain wateriness in the lower belly, and a feculence of mucus rammed up both nostrils, not unlike two small coral reefs.

As he paced he kept looking at his watch, feeling time course away from him, while he remained imprisoned in a permanent, embarrassed agony of the present. It was the window of Smith's that snapped him out of it, provided the visual salts. A rack of copies of the *Radio Times* was positioned so as to grab the attention of passers-by. It grabbed Richard all right, grabbed him like a street fighter grabbing a collar, thrusting a belligerent face into a cowering one. But it wasn't *a* face, it was faces. Bell's faces, serried ranks of Bells, a tintinnabulation of them resounding in Richard's head. Below each smiling visage was a version of his ever mutable slogan: 'Can You Ring Me?'

Richard resolved compromise. He got back on the tube and headed into town. Getting out at Tottenham Court Road he walked along to a menswear store and bought a pair of black chinos, a black blazer, a black pullover shirt, clean underwear and socks. He couldn't afford all of it really, but also couldn't stand not to look presentable, Ursula-worthy.

Richard slid into the Sealink at five to seven, and ducked along the corridor to the gents'. Here he shaved with nose-hair-paring exactitude. He also crouched in one of the stalls, to swab the grooves of his body with wads of moistened toilet paper, before scrabbling at the cellophane packaging and wrapping himself in his new finery. Five more minutes in front of the mirror – ignoring the comments of Sealink regulars as they filed past him to snort, scratch and sniff – and Richard was as ready as he'd ever be. He advanced along the corridor, towards the bar, at a steady trot. A Norman knight at Agincourt.

The first arrow came barrelling down vertically on him from the barman, Julius. Richard entered the bar, sidled up to the bar, put his elbow on the bar, and undertook the subtle business of gaining the barman's attention. This took about fifteen minutes. Finally the orange divot was in front of Richard and he essayed the following casual enquiry: 'Julius – seen Ursula?'

'No,' came the reply, the 'N' riving him from occiput to nape, the 'o' set alight and dropping neatly around his neck. *Not here?* It was now ten past seven – she *had* to be here. Was she toying with him?

'I'll have – ' but the orange divot was gone, to the other end of the bar, to serve an actor whose most impressive credit to date was the voiceover for a Pepto-Bismol advert.

Richard ranged the Sealink Club with the loping, multijointed gait of a maddened polar bear. He charged upstairs, fell downstairs, looked in the brasserie-style cafeteria, the cafeteria-style brasserie, the table-football room; he even called her name several times outside the ladies', softly, every bit of him agitated but pitching it low, in three quavering syllables, 'Uuuur-suuuu-laaa . . .', until two hack-harridans emerged, knock-kneed with merriment – charged on his account.

Then he was back in the bar for a while, clenching and

unclenching his hands around fictive balls of hard, realistically rubber anxiety. Richard didn't want Kelburn, Reiser, Slatter and all the others to turn up before her – it was unthinkable. He'd be sucked straight back down that plughole of loathsomeness, which connected directly to the sewer of the previous night. He must at least speak with Ursula alone before this happened. He had to capitalise on the Post-it note.

Richard thought of the private room he and Reiser had been in the evening before. Could she be up there? One of the chambermaids who serviced the room had also been serviced by Bell. Richard found it hard to credit, but the experience indebted her to him. She made sure that a copy of the key was available for Bell, or any of his cronies, when they required sequestration from the rest of the club.

If Ursula was up there, what could she possibly be doing? The long day of speculation, insecurity and hair-trigger lust was beginning to tell on Richard. He contemplated lurid images of Ursula going down – on Reiser! On Slatter! On Kelburn! On still weasellier, greasier members of the clique. As the phantom figures mounted one another in his mind, Richard mounted the stairs. By the time he reached the fifth floor his heart was pounding, his visual field expanded and contracted, a squeezebox of perception. Without pausing to summon himself he straight-palmed the door open.

It crashed back on its hinges to reveal that a small gate-leg table had been set up in the very centre of the room; around this four figures were grouped playing cards. From their clothing and the set of their bodies, Richard recognised the clique members Reiser, Slatter, Kelburn and Mearns – the greenmailer. But when their faces turned to the source of the interruption, Richard saw four sets of near-identical features. Each of them had the same thick-set neck, the same jutting jaw, the same high, white forehead, the same red lips and broad-bridged nose. It was a group of Bells – a belfry. Four sets of black eyes examined Richard for a long, long fraction of a second. They bored into him, as if he were a diseased liver on which they were keen to do a biopsy.

The sight of the belfry was so incomprehensible, so weird, that Richard fell back against the wall of the corridor, mouthing – rather than saying – 'What the fu – '. He rubbed his eyes; he felt dizzy, nauseous, as if about to faint. He sank to his knees.

Then a firm hand grasped Richard's shoulder, and a

firm — yet soft — voice clasped his ear: 'What's the matter, Richard?' Richard shook his head, his vision cleared, he looked up into the black eyes, began to recoil — but this time it was the real Bell, the authentic Bell. 'Come on, come in here.' Bell lifted Richard up under the arms. Lifted him as easily as another man might pick up a free newspaper, as a prelude to throwing it in a dustbin. It was the first time the big man had touched Richard, and he found it disconcertingly thrilling — Bell was so strong, so adamant.

Bell dropped Richard in an armchair inside the room. The others had left off their card game. They were still twisted round in their seats, but they no longer had the appearance of Bell clones. They had their own faces back, their own, leering faces. Todd Reiser stood up, brushing the outsize ash-fragments of a joint from his little lap, and said, 'All right now, young Richard? You were out for the count there for a moment . . .'

'I'm — I'm fine, really. Fine. Just took the stairs too fast.'

'Not feeling the pace, are we young Richard? Too many late nights, too much *fun*?' This was sneered. Reiser couldn't *do* concern.

'N-no, really. It was the stairs, and then seeing you all . . . You all looked like . . .'

'What?' This was from Slatter, who was openly worrying a cuticle with yellow teeth. 'What did we look like?'

'Y-you all looked like . . .' – Richard indicated the big man, who was now standing over by the window – '. . . like Bell.'

The room exploded in laughter, different varieties of sarcastic cackling, all the way from Slatter's wheezing, nominal 'Hugh-hugh-hugh- ' to Reiser's exploitative, pronominal 'Her-her-her-her-'; even Bell heaved a little. Richard was still too dazed to be shamed by this; he was running over the past minute or so in his mind, again and again. Had there really been four Bells in the room? Or had it just appeared that way? After all, Bell's ubiquity was undeniable; and if Richard was going to have a hallucination, it was fairly likely to incorporate the man whose actions, whose thoughts, obsessed him. If it hadn't been Bell, who else but –

'Ursula!' cried Mearns, the greenmailer. 'How lovely to see you; you look quite, quite marvellous.' He rose and went to meet her. Richard unstuck his head from his hands and blinked. She was standing in the doorway, bracing herself with both hands held above her head. She had one thigh raised up and half-crossed over the top of the other. She was wearing some sort of golden, spangled top, the spangles scattered over a fine mesh that exposed as much as it concealed her magnificent *embonpoint*. And Ursula wasn't just wearing a short skirt, she was wearing a pelmet – a little flange of thick, green, brocaded material that hung down, barely covering her lower abdomen. To either side of this lappet, flaring curtains of material descended. If Ursula had been straight-legged, ordinarily disposed, this would have presented a decorous enough picture. However, given the attitude she had struck, the longer drapes of cloth fell away, making an arch that framed the very juncture of her thighs. Richard let fly with a deep, glottal groan.

This was ignored by the others, who all rose and went over to Ursula. One by one they all kissed the air some inches in front of her cheek, as exemplary an acknowledgement as possible of the fact that they would rather be some inches *inside* her body.

Richard looked on from where he was slumped. Would she give some indication that she was sorry to have missed their rendezvous, that this was an unwanted and hateful turn of events? She did, in the form of lifting

up the fingers of one hand, pushing them in his direction, and chafing the two middle ones together.

Much, much later that evening, the clique were
encabbed and heading east. There had been some
calls for a trip to a restaurant, but Mearns – whose
party, after all, it was – had already had dinner with
Pablo (the clique's preferred euphemism – this month –
for doing cocaine), and couldn't be bothered, as he put it,
with 'paying x quid cover charge, x quid service charge,
and twenty-bloody-x for food to play patty-cake with
– rather than eat'. Once the other cliquers had snacked
with Mr Escobar as well, they didn't argue.

Mearns's greenmail party had begun the same way
as any other cliquey evening at the Sealink, continued
the same way as any cliquey evening at the Sealink,
and was now speedily moving towards a dénouement
of crushing obviousness: they were going to Limehouse
to smoke opium.

Bell was up front, speaking to the cab driver. Richard
and Mearns sat in the back, either side of Ursula, while
the others were following in another cab. It had taken
masterly powers of anticipation, of jockeying, for
Richard to get this close to Ursula. Not that she

was ignoring Richard any more than usual – she was simply ignoring him.

The cabbie – who was a middle-aged Syrian man with a Colonel Blimpish moustache, beach-ball paunch and shattered air – was telling Bell a long and involved story, haltingly and with real feeling, about his imprisonment and torture for an attempt on the life of President Assad. Bell appeared to be concentrating deeply on the story. He studied the cabbie's pained face intently, nodding, uttering tiny, encouraging grunts. But it was difficult for Richard to hear everything, because the radio was on and tuned to Bell's own phone-in show. This, as usual, was being dominated by Bell, berating callers, inciting callers, ignoring callers. The broadcast Bell and the in-car Bell stood proxy for each other.

Richard thought it queer, but Ursula and Mearns seemed not to have noticed. He was telling her about the last time he'd smoked opium, with triplet thirteen-year-old prostitutes in Patpong. Richard could feel Ursula's ribs move against his when she sniggered. The fulsome aroma of Jicki was thick in the enclosed atmosphere. If there had been a Magic Tree car air-freshener that distilled the odour of Ursula, it would have been called 'Fuck Fragrance'. Richard's cock was like an iron girder some pile-driver had rammed into his crotch. He tried to concentrate on what the driver was saying. It was a tale of courage, warmth and fortitude in the face of craven, cold brutality. The cabbie had been an air-force general. He had been befriended by Assad's brother. There had been high-living times in Switzerland. Tarts and Krug. The general had become disgusted by the decadence. He had fomented a coup. He'd ended up in jail for twelve years. Beaten on the feet. Beaten on the balls. Screwed up by his thumbs.

The juxtaposition of this and the squealing, coked-up atmosphere that had prevailed among the clique since they left the Sealink was grotesque. Richard felt sickened. Bell went on nodding sympathetically. The cab oozed across town. As they stopped by the lights at the junction with Kingsland Road, Richard looked to his left to see, framed between the concrete stanchion of a bus stop and the quivering bum of a double-decker, a lingerie advert that featured a young woman of such astonishing, bursting pulchritude (her mons, her nipples straining, yet demure) that Richard feared for his trousers.

But beyond the bus stop, in a door adrift with litter, sat a double amputee drinking a can of Enigma lager.

Richard looked deep into the stumps levelled in his direction, capped off with leather stump-protectors. Or, as Richard thought to himself, footless boots. He tried to imagine his cock amputated, a leather stump-protector grinding into his groin. He sensed his twanging erection subside a little. The cab oozed on.

The two vehicles carrying Bell's clique arrived at Milligan Street, behind the Limehouse Causeway, at exactly the same time, and their occupants debouched into the windy road. Things had got drizzly in London – as they often do; a chilly, wet tongue of leaf blew against Richard's cheek. He looked up to see no tree, but the Legoland edifice of Canary Wharf looming overhead, its aircraft-warning beacon making a dim, provincial disco of the metropolitan night. Bell gave his account number to the cabbie, signed the clipboard where the formerly-screwed thumb indicated. Once Assad's failed assassin had driven off, Richard said to Bell, 'What did you think of that? Pretty amazing story.'

'What story?'

'About Assad, about Syria – what the cabbie was saying.'

'Oh that – to be frank I wasn't paying much attention; I wanted to listen to tonight's show.

There could be comeback over what I said about wassername.'

'Who?'

'That soap star.'

Bell broke away from Richard and mounted the short flight of stairs to the door of the house in front of them. Richard turned to Ursula, who was coming up behind. 'Did you hear what the cabbie was saying? Any of it?'

'What?'

'About Assad, about torture?' Richard couldn't believe that he was getting carried away like this, that he was attempting to pierce the superficial skin of the evening.

'Yeah, some. Grisly, huh?' Ursula groped in her bag for a cigarette. Her jaw worked, chewing the cocaine cud of nothing.

'I should say so. It's awful to think of things like that happening in the world, and we just go on talking about *nothing*, doing *nothing*, just writing on the wallpaper. Doesn't it make you feel sick sometimes?'

Ursula's jaw stopped working for a moment. She gave Richard a level stare. He looked into her eyes and saw there what he was always looking for: that she understood. That she really understood. That she

knew this wasted go-round was just that; and that she
– like Richard – had higher aspirations. Aspirations to
a life that might appear dull, conventional, to Bell and
his clique, but which was in fact full of love, security,
trust – the important values. Ursula reached out a hand
and gently rumpled Richard's blond curls. 'You know
what?' she said.

'W-what?'

'You're sweet.'

The old Chinaman who let them into the mouldering
house seemed to be well known to Bell. He asked after
the man's grandchildren, made reference to certain
mutual business acquaintances. While this went on
the rest of the clique remained backed up in the
vestibule. Eventually they all shuffled on in. It was a
warped, early-nineteenth-century house. At one time
it would have been part of the old Limehouse rookery, a
teeming, tri-dimensional dying space of interconnected
alleys, courtyards and tenements; but now it stood alone,
carved out from the past, teetering on the edge of the
Docklands Enterprise Zone.

The Chinaman led them through rooms that had
not so much been decorated, as arrived naturally at a

bewildering number of styles. Some were hung with Persian carpets, others had pop posters tacked on the walls, still more were strip-lit and tiled, like toilets or Moroccan cafés. Everywhere the atmosphere was dank, dilapidated; and everywhere there were people taking drugs. Two Iranians sat on phallic bolsters, moodily chasing the dragon; on a velveteen-covered divan a gaggle of giggling upper-class girls – as out of their element as gorillas in Regent's Park – were high on E, stroking each other's hair; and as the clique climbed the stairs, they passed two black guys smoking crack in a pipe made from a Volvic bottle. 'I prefer Evian myself,' Mearns sneered as they tromped by.

'Whassit t'you, cunt?' came back at him; but the speaker's companion muttered, 'Safe, Danny,' and they let it lie.

Later, Richard could barely recall the actual opium-smoking. It had taken place in an attic room, the sloping ceiling forcing the cliquers into a series of staggered postures, from upright to crouched to supine. The Chinaman spawned a daughter – or granddaughter, or great-granddaughter – who looked about eleven, and who did the business of priming the pipe, passing it round, cleaning out the dross, repeating the operation.

Richard glared at Ursula, who was allowing Bell to cup the back of her head and guide the pipe's thick stem into her mouth. The image had an awful implication. Richard concentrated on the cracked paint of the skirting board, the furring of dust on the lampshade. Outside in the street a dog was shouting at a barking drunk. The thick, sweet, organic smoke filled the room. Like agitated children being given a narcotic bedtime narrative, the cliquers were calmed as it did the rounds.

Then, the black guy from the stairs crashed in, smacked Mearns in the mouth and ran out. There was less pandemonium than might have been expected. Bell exited the room and found the Chinaman, who in turn got hold of his minder, a big Maltese guy called Vince whose nose had been cut in half and badly sewn together again.

The Chinaman ushered them all back down through the warren of rooms, with much solicitous cooing. Bell was saying 'No matter . . . No matter . . .' in such a way, Richard understood, as to make the Chinaman feel that it mattered a great deal, and that something *had* to be done.

More cabs were waiting outside – someone must

have used their mobile. The clique encabbed. As they pulled away from the house Richard saw the black guy. He was halfway down the area steps, and Vince appeared to be throttling him. Or perhaps – and the thought came to Richard as painfully as a sick bubble of gaseous indigestion squeezes between waist and band – Vince was making love to him, and cutting off his carotid artery as a means of inducing shattering orgasm.

Then the Sealink again – the table-football room, to be precise. The club had bought an outsize table-football table from a paedophile member – of parliament. Now, the wannabe macho and the never gonnabe macho flexed their tethered cocks, yanked, biffed and slammed the balls. Taking up an unobtrusive position against one wall of the room, Richard got trapped behind two seats of agitated suit trousers, whose owners were – to all intents and purposes – psychically merged with the battered eight-inch figurines of cockless men that they manipulated.

Bell was over by the bar, talking to Trellet, an influential, older-generation member of the clique. Trellet was a comic actor who had made quite dumb amounts of money by impersonating a bumbling, lovable paterfamilias in an endless sitcom. In fact,

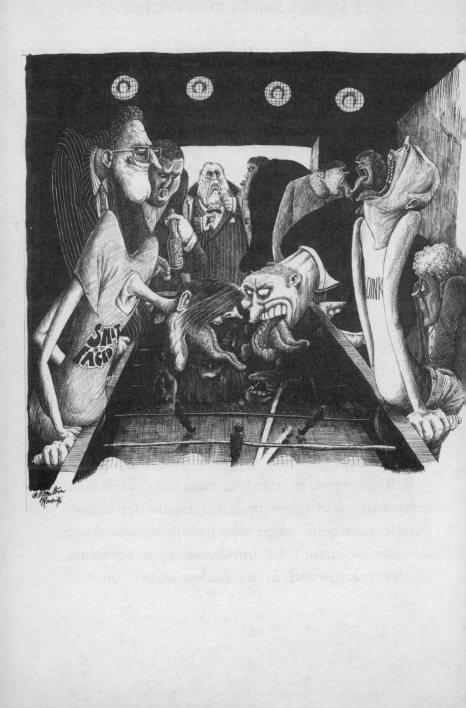

as soon as there was a wrap, Trellet's face collapsed from the expansively benign to the pettily vicious. In appearance not unlike a pocket-sized Robert Morley (*circa Beat the Devil*), Trellet was possessed of appetites as sluttish as Bell's, but with an added full twist of genuine perversion.

Right now, Richard couldn't forbear from listening to them. As he did so his delicate ears, networked with the finest of bluest of veins, changed from the white-pink of shame to the deep, angry pink of impotence and anger. Trellet was telling two anecdotes with intersecting themes, which converged on his drive to humiliate anyone who crossed his path.

The first anecdote featured an aristocratic girl, crazed by cocaine, whom Trellet had forced to lick kitchen tiling, lick herself, lick him – in order to get the merest lick of cocaine. The second was more in the manner of a revelation. Trellet – it was unfolded with nauseating aplomb – kept a Down's Syndrome adolescent mistress (this was *dignifying* it – obviously sex slave would have been nearer the truth), in a flat on the far side of Battersea Bridge. Trellet, jowls bunching, contorting with delight, gave details of domestic arrangements, and then more forced accommodations.

Ursula Bentley leant against the banisters, a Venus in spangles, trails of her long, dark brown hair twining around her upper body, forming a growing bodice. The good thing about opium is that when you're on it only the things that matter, matter. Or so thought Richard as he gathered himself together, and made the supreme effort of not registering the fact that Trellet was extending visiting privileges – 'You wouldn't believe it mate, her mouth's that sloppy, that *gooey*.' Richard got upright. He walked around the table-football table to where Ursula stood, put a firm hand on her shoulder and said, 'I'm going to get a cab now – perhaps you should let me get one for you as well?'

He was as surprised as he would have been had she at that point brokered an IRA ceasefire when Ursula smiled and said, 'Yes.'

On the night of Mearns's greenmail party Richard ended up taking the cab all the way back to Ursula's flat in Kensington with her. She rumpled his curls once more, said he was 'sweet', pecked him near the cheek, and didn't demur when he suggested that they have lunch together at some unspecified time in the future. It wasn't until the cab pulled away that Richard realised he had only a tenner plus some change in his pocket.

Ursula, typically, hadn't ventured a contribution, and he had no plastic or chequebook. The cabbie took him as far as Notting Hill before turfing him out, and Richard walked on from there.

Walked on through a distempered ground mist, across the Portobello Road, and up past the Front Line, where even at this hour the crack-heads were gathered in knots of desperation on the corner by the bookie's, their eyes tracking the passing cars like the targeting laser beams of ground-to-crack missiles. Richard knew what they were, what they wanted. He identified with them more than they could ever possibly know.

He reached Hornsey well after dawn, his body swathed in clashing, contrasting colours of narcosis: blue, red, purple; up, down, zigzag; but despite it all he still had the groin-borne horn, was still thinking about Ursula, imagining her in any number of poses and postures, naked, clothed, her limbs bent back, or even amputated – like the piss-head in the East End doorway – so as to aid more effective penetration. Yet when bed got to Richard, he found that he was spent with lust, that he could no longer either summon her up or contain himself. After three strokes, he came like a beer belly spluttering in a pub toilet – great gouts of spunk that drenched his doll's-house duvet. Needless to say, he didn't make it in to *Rendezvous* later that morning.

Autumn quit London, a transient, seasonal tourist clad in leaves of tan Burberry, and left the city behind to endure its own chill, its own immemorial, hibernatory dolour.

Every dog has his day, and Richard Hermes succeeded the glove fetishist as the Preview Editor of *Rendezvous*. His new job accorded him some perks, including the speedy advancement of his candidature for election to the Sealink Club. It now took him only five, instead of fifteen, minutes to get a drink from Julius. He also moved further towards the eye, the howling vacuity, at the epicentre of Bell's clique. He was included as a matter of course in the phone rounds that preceded clique meetings. He was patronised and humiliated as much as the others – but no longer more so.

On nights when he couldn't find the wherewithal, the energy, to meet them at this or that restaurant, or bar, or club, he would get calls from crackly mobiles: 'Richard . . . Yah, it's me, Bell. We were just thinking that there's one thing really missing from the evening.

Ursula's here and she's feeling a bit . . . I dunno . . . a bit overcome. She says she really just wants to see you – '

'Really! Where are you?'

'We're in this place . . . Slatter, what's this place?' The sound of tittering, guffawing, no exchange of information that Richard's straining ear could detect, and then: 'Yeah, it's a Greek joint on the Finch – ' Then invariably the line would go dead, leaving Richard in hellish limbo, not knowing whether to go through the *Yellow Pages* looking for every correlation of 'Greek restaurant' and the single first syllable 'Finch', or simply to butt his head against the wall until unconsciousness, unconscious-of-Ursulaness, set in.

And sometimes calls would come really late at night, at three, four, or five, after Richard had left Ursula at home (which he was now permitted to do – and pay for), or still out with the clique. He would be dreaming, chasing her along some Mediterranean strand, when the insistent trill would pull him back to the sweaty confines of his bed, yank him up, yank the receiver up – 'Y-yeah – who'ssat?' – only for his ear to be met with the evil purr of the dialling tone, and, when he tried 1471, with the chilling, robotic information 'You were called today at four-forty-five hours; sorry, we do not have the number . . .' It was the 'sorry' that was the killer; for, if the recorded voice *were truly* sorry, it was the most sympathy that Richard had ever received for his predicament.

Things got worse in some ways and better in others. The activities of Bell and his clique were as vicious, sophomoric and cynical as ever, but at the same time Richard's suit of Ursula was progressing, albeit at the pace of a snail on Tuinal. They had lunch together most weeks in a sandwich bar equidistant from her flat and the offices of *Rendezvous*. On these occasions her entire manner was different, she was the Ursula he wanted . . . he wanted . . . he wanted to make his wife. She preferred tuna and mayonnaise on brown bread, while he invariably had salami on rye.

Gone was the terminal merriment of her evening self, the louche demeanour, flash of leg, side of breast, whisper of pudenda. Gone was the coke fakeover, the lips red as ketchup, the eyes sparkling like crystals on a mirror. Gone too was that scent, that sweet, ineffable, seductive perfume. The one that Richard associated with her, as surely as he associated gravity with the earth. And with the scent gone she was more approachable, more girl-next-door than was altogether credible.

She was skittish, coltish, vouchsafing little gobbets of her past, a past that was wholly charming to Richard, matching as it did his own in most respects: a father she loved, but felt distanced from by divorce; a mother whose influence she was still attempting to shake off; siblings who would come up to the city to enjoy her giddy round, and then berate her for her lack of conviction, application, seriousness. She and Richard would commiserate with each other, mull over each other's petty miseries and dissatisfactions. Richard would even discuss her latest column, without in any way averring – even to himself – that what she wrote had all the mondial impact of a used cotton bud falling on to a damp towel.

But on these occasions Bell and the clique would never be mentioned, and when they met up again, that evening or the next in the bar of the Sealink, it would be neglect as usual. The same old brackish badinage, the same cruel jokes. And Ursula would behave as if the lunches never took place, as if there was no link between the two worlds they now inhabited.

There was also a further, more unsettling downside. As cold infiltrated the city, taking possession first of the foundations of the buildings, and then of successive storeys, working its way up until chill of earth and chill of sky effected union, so the press beanos, the book launches, the première parties reached new heights of purposeless frenzy. The members of the clique weren't simply having dinner with Pablo now, they were also having tea most days, lunch on some, and even the occasional, high-powered, breakfast meeting.

This was because in early November the clique had acquired a new cocaine dealer, courtesy of Slatter. This individual was a Slatteralike, so dusted with 'druff that it was hard not to imagine that some of his product had escaped its packaging to form an unorthodox mini-piste. But on the plus side, his tackle was always of the best – creamy white, rocky, unstepped on – and he turned up whenever and wherever, at the touch of a few rubberised buttons. So frequently, indeed, did Richard call upon the dealer's services (usually at Ursula's behest) that he soon ascended the ranking of frequent callers programmed into the dealer's mobile, until he was well up in the top ten of the snort parade.

Richard was doing so much cocaine now that the numbers that should have been intaglioed into the back of his credit card were embossed, raised up like the word 'POLO' on the eponymous mint – only back to front.

Richard was doing so much cocaine now that some mornings the rigid mucilage in his nostrils couldn't be shifted, even with a sharp nail and generous sluicings of salted warm water. He seriously considered going down to the mews garage at the end of his road and asking the surly mechanic there to rebore his nose to a higher calibre.

Richard was doing so much cocaine now that he never worried about getting involuntary erections; instead he worried about ever getting another erection at all.

But most disturbingly of all, the increased cocaine consumption brought with it more of what Richard termed – in order to take some of the sinister sting out of them – *belles époques*. These were those veridical occurrences – like the one he had had at the Sealink on the evening of Mearns's greenmail party – when he thought he saw Bell's familiar features, but then looked again to discover that it was some other cliquer who was withering at him.

Walking up Old Compton Street one grey, hungover morning, he saw Bell's broad back bent low over the public phone in the gay café on the corner of Frith Street. Richard was surprised to see the big man out this early, and as he approached the back – fashionably suited by Barries in the finest of hound's-tooth checks – he checked and rechecked, to be sure. He even worked his way around the horizon of dark brow very slowly, very carefully, as a space probe might make its way over the curvature of an alien planet, in order to be certain that he wasn't committing some awful solecism.

But it was definitely Bell. The flesh had that exact Bell shade, like the inside lip of an old Wedgwood teacup, and the black bangs arched over in exactly the right way. The hand that grasped receiver against ear even had Bell's signet ring on its fourth finger. Richard said 'Hiyah!' brightly, but somewhere between the 'Hi' and the 'yah' the figure on the phone turned, and as the face came into view there was an instant when two sets of features were revealed to Richard simultaneously: those of Bell, and those of someone else. Then the Bell features dissolved and he was looking straight into Trellet's face. The venal thespian expostulated, 'What the fuck are you doing? Grabbing hold of me like that – get off!'

Richard reeled away, back into the street. His head pounded. He wasn't so much humiliated as painfully disoriented, perplexed. There was that – and there was the oppressive smell of Jicki in the air. Why was Trellet wearing the fragrance Richard associated solely with Ursula? There was no particular reason why he shouldn't, but it did seem a bizarre coincidence.

Then there was the occasion when Richard had arranged to meet Todd Reiser for some sushi in the little café in the basement of the Japanese Centre on Brewer Street. Richard was late. That morning had been one of the worst – hangover-wise – he could remember. His nose had bled when he blew it over the soapdish-sized sink in his Hornsey flat; and then he'd fainted, banging his head hard on the radiator as he went down. Richard hadn't even bothered to go into *Rendezvous*; he'd simply sent a 'sick' fax from the bureau on the corner of his road. His co-workers weren't that taken aback – they already had a slew of the things, which they'd pinned to a photograph of Richard up on the office bulletin board. Pinned to his nose, to be precise.

Cramped and bent, he had come down the narrow flight of stairs to the sushi bar. Hunched over one of the lacquered boxes of fish niblets was – Bell! But as Richard descended, and Bell's chopsticks ascended to his sculpted lips, the big man seemed to shimmer, to dissolve, like a reflection in agitated water, the transmogrification was effected that quickly. In Bell's place sat Todd Reiser, grinning facetiously.

Richard gulped, heaved. The lingering scent of Jicki was in the air, with its faintly sticky *mélange* of fruits and flowers. Richard said nothing, moved past Reiser and went straight to the toilet, where he had an *hors d'œuvre* with Pablo.

But most of the *belles époques* occurred at the Sealink – and occurred with a mounting rhythm. Whenever Richard ran into any of the clique members off guard, in the brasserie, the restaurant, the table-football room or either of the bars, he would see them first as Bell and only latterly as themselves. And always there was the smell of Jicki, the smell of Ursula.

Richard would have been more disturbed by all of this had it not been for the fact that he knew he was getting closer to Ursula, closer to making her his. She now allowed him to kiss her full on both cheeks when they met, and near the perfect bow of her lips when they parted. Day by day, party by party, line of coke by line of coke, Richard's mouth drew closer to Ursula's. He knew that she liked him; she made it abundantly clear. She had stopped talking of her sexual affairs in his presence — something he was grateful for. In the past she had referred to them deliberately, coldly, as if assaying the exact quantities of bile and envy she could engender in him. But now she would often back out when the clique's prattling became prurient, take Richard by the arm and draw him away.

Richard also knew he was on a slippery slope. Things at work were getting sticky. The Editor had told him flatly to buck up his attendance, and get both himself and his pages to bed earlier, or else there would be some radical downsizing of Richard's career prospects in the new year. The Editor lectured Richard quite severely, made reference to sightings of him with Bell's clique in the Sealink. '*He* may be able to run through life at that kind of pace,' he said, squinting at Richard through his absurd, pentagonal, designer spectacles, 'but he's pulling down two hundred grand a year and filing x thousand words a week . . .' — the pause hung in the inefficiently filtered air; Richard thought, I'm a sick, sick man, in a sick, sick building — '. . . and what are *you* for?'

Richard was, he decided, 'for' being tormented by Bell. Although he had come to despise Bell and everything he stood for, he couldn't stop himself sticking to the tacky man. It was getting to the point where Richard's revulsion from Bell was becoming physical as well. He no longer contemplated that massive, dense body with anything like awe or curiosity; instead it frankly disturbed him. The thought of the texture of Bell stubble, the heft of Bellflesh, the odour of Bellfluents and Bellsecretions was foul. The idea of touching the fingers that had typed all those bigoted opinions, those tendentious assertions, those unwarranted insinuations! Of pressing to one's own lips the waspish lips that had uttered such slanders, and feeling the tongue loaded with venom press against your own!

Richard dreamed this – and woke up screaming in the cold, clammy, winter predawn.

As if both to engender and to bank up this malaise, Bell's media ubiquity had never been so evident to Richard. There seemed to be more and more of the billboards advertising the phone-in show. There was one on Charing Cross Road, one in the Strand. After the one on the Euston Road – which Richard invariably passed on his undulant cab rides home at three, four and five in the morning – there was a chain of the damn things, like beacons of reminder taunting him back to Hornsey.

If Richard chanced to pick up an old copy of the *Standard* while on the tube, it was always folded so as to display Bell's column. This was set out in a series of snide little paragraphs such as: 'No need to ask why the fragrant Jasmine Phillips is taking such an interest in the resident combo at Grindley's Upstairs. After all, it's a jazz band – and our Jasmine can't go for long without blowing someone's trumpet . . .' In between each of these casual calumnies, acting as a running subhead, was the single piece of onomatopoeia 'BONG!'. No one was ever saved by this Bell – only sacrificed to the alienation and indifference of five million commuters.

Bell's chat show was put on an extended pre-Christmas run. Every night the Minotaur sat in his plastic labyrinth of a studio and drew his 'guests' into querulous quadrilles. A repeat of each show was also screened the following morning, so that inattentive viewers, addicted to the remote, would find themselves breathing the Bellosphere, and jump-cutting the very fabric of space-time itself, along with their thaumaturge.

Richard thought of home and going there. His father, a retired solicitor, would enjoy seeing him. They would play chess, and walk across the sodden fields to the local pub for a pint, while his stepmother put on the dinner. His father's retriever would scamper ahead, rooting in the hedgerows. His father's pipe smoke would bunch and coil in the night air. They would discuss what had happened in London fully and frankly. His father would turn out to have hidden reserves of wisdom concerning people like Bell and the things that they did. As the first draught of real ale gushed into Richard's mouth, he would feel it bringing with it a more real, more tangible world than the febrile machinations of Bell and the clique. There would be turkey for Christmas dinner, and plenty of stuffing.

This vision came to him in the urinals beneath Notting Hill Gate, and when it cleared Richard found that he had toppled forward so that the side of his face and his shoulder were pressed against the slick jaundice of the splashback. The toilet attendant was shaking him. 'Don't leave yer cock dangling out of yer flies 'ere, mate,' he advised. 'Some cunt 'll have it off you an' it'll be on sale in the Porterbeller before you can say Errol Flynn!'

Richard resolved to quit London the day after the *Rendezvous* office party. But before he did so he would make one last assault on Mount Ursula. If he failed

he would accept it, move on, break with Bell, turn his attention to higher things, dust off his ideals and reignite his ambition.

He phoned her in the dead hour after what would have been his lunch break, had he made it into the office that morning. 'Ursula?'

'Yeah?'

'It's Richard.'

'Richard – how nice to hear from you. Are you coming out to Kelburn's country place at the weekend? Apparently he's got some MDMA fresh from Sandoz in Switzerland, we're all going to go bacchanalian.'

'I dunno. I thought I might go to my dad's place on Friday. Christmas you know.'

'Yeah, yeah, you're right, I ought to think about that – '

'And frankly, Ursula, I think I've had enough of Kelburn.'

'I know what you mean.'

'Ursula.'

'Yeah?'

'I'd like to see you before I go.'

'I'll be in the club this evening, I'm meeting – '

'Alone, Ursula, I want to see you alone.' He could

hear her breathing on the other end of the phone. He imagined the warm curvature of her breast rising and falling, pressing into its fabric mould.

Then she replied, 'I'd like to see you alone as well, Richard.'

'Shall we have dinner, then? On Thursday, just the two of us?'

'Yeah, OK, pick me up from here and we'll avoid the Sealink altogether. I was meant to be having dinner with Bell and some TV producer in from LA, but they can just do without me.'

After hanging up Richard went to the gents' toilet, locked himself into a cubicle, confronted the commode, voided himself, then sprinkled three-quarters of a gram of cocaine on top of the excreta. He prayed over this powdery, maculate offering, prayed for success with Ursula, and wagered his soul as the stake.

Three days later it was a very different Richard Hermes who rang the entryphone outside Ursula Bentley's flat. The cocaine had fallen away from him like a conning tower blown off the side of a Saturn Five. Without Pablo extending dining privileges, Richard's psyche soared. He had put on a spurt of work, tidied up his flat, renegotiated his overdraft, and telephoned both of his parents. He felt as virtuous as a nonagenarian nun, nodding away her virginal life in some closed order. He felt – somewhat paradoxically – ready for love.

They ate at the Brasserie St Quentin, opposite the Brompton Oratory. Ursula was demure to begin with, in her lunching mode. There was no talk of Bell, of the clique. Richard was nervous but steady. He acquitted himself well with the waiters and the wine list. By the time they got on to the main course (or at any rate *he* did – Ursula had confined herself to an entrée of Parmesan shavings atop rocket leaves, and was going for more of the same), he felt he was hitting his stride. She was laughing at his jokes, making her own conversational sallies; once or twice her knee brushed against his beneath the table.

Ursula was more beautiful than ever this evening. She was wearing a velvet variation on the little black dress, black suede high heels, and sepia-toned stockings. Richard knew they were stockings because of the seams he had followed into the Brasserie, seams he wanted to follow to their ultimate end. Her breasts rose and fell in the soft vice of the velvet bodice. Her brown locks were piled on top of her head in tawny cumulation.

Her brown eyes, with their flecks of gold, contemplated him in a way he hadn't seen before; an amused, frankly sensual way.

But despite all this, it came as a profound shock to Richard when, after he had ordered their coffee, she leant forward, exposing her breasts to him, cupped her slim hand over his, and said, 'Let's not have a *digestif* here – I've got some brandy Bell gave me back at the flat . . .' The odour of Jicki came off her like musk off a lioness.

Richard's hand shot up to re-summon the only recently departed waiter. 'C–could we have the bill, please?' he stuttered like Oliver in the workhouse.

How could he have imagined that she was rich? The flat Ursula admitted Richard to was no bigger than his own, just a large room with a kitchenette at one end and a bathroom at the other. A tall, dirty-paned window bleared out on to that cosmically awful, incarnated oxymoron: a lightwell.

There were a few obvious sticks of furniture: a collapsing sofabed, an armchair, a chest of drawers. Spilling from cupboards, tented over the arms of chairs, lying in huddles on the floor were elements of the fantastic costume she assumed in her Sealink persona: the microskirts, the scintillating body stockings, the slinky boob–tubes. A pair of tights was flung over the shade of a table lamp, although whether to mute the lighting or not, Richard could not have said.

And over all of this scene, like gunsmoke over no man's land, wafted the pungency of Jicki, so strong that Richard could almost see molecules of bergamot and lavender fizzing and boiling in the room's close atmosphere.

She got the bottle of brandy from the kitchenette. She swilled some water round in two dusty tumblers and then poured each of them four of her slim fingers. She stepped off the platform of her heels and moved across the room. She footled with some buttons on a console, and the voice of Tricky's Martine welled from a hidden speaker: 'You sure you wanna be with me – I've nothing to give / When there's trust there'll be treats, when we funk we'll hear beats . . .' The trip–hop tripped and hopped. Ursula put her statuesque body down on the plinth of the sofabed and patted the faded nap by her smooth haunch. Richard joined her.

To begin with he felt awkward; the jacket of his best suit nipped him under his arms; but after he took

84

her in those arms they felt nothing but her, the massed voluptuousness of her. Then his mouth was over hers, pressuring the infinitely sweet tackiness of marinaded lips. This occurred so naturally that it seemed a wholly mutual seduction. Her tongue came into his mouth and he introduced his to hers. Grass snake twined with viper.

There was no fumbling, no awkwardness as his hands roamed over her, cupping her breast, cupping her hip, stroking the slick surfaces of her thighs.

They were lying half across the sofabed now. Her hands tugged at his waist, pushing up his shirt. They were cool – her palms – cool wavelets on the baking salt pan of his stomach. He moaned into her mouth. She moaned into his. Martine moaned to both of them. His fingers worried up the hem of her dress. He felt the brocade at the top of her stockings, and then he was home free. He couldn't believe the softness of her flesh. He couldn't believe the sensation of silk over pubic hair, over parted lips.

They divested themselves. She simply sat upright, crossed her arms in front of her, and pulled the dress over her head. Her bra and pants were ivory satin. She was a lucid wet dream sitting there right in front of him.

It was as if by wanking for night after night after night, her image before him, Richard had made a spare rib – of his spare prick.

He got his trousers off, his shirt off. He smiled at her, but she wasn't in the mood for it, she just pulled his head back down to hers. His fingers went to her nipples, teased them, pinched them. She gasped. His hands then ranged south, pulled down the ligature of her pants. He grasped her vulva as if it was a scruff. 'Fuck me,' she said, 'please fuck me.' She freed his cock. Her hands were dry ice. He groaned throatily, half rose, stripped the last leaves from her sapling body. She lay back bucking and writhing. She grasped him again, guided him into her.

As soon as Richard felt himself engulfed by her, he realised that he would be able to manage at best three strokes without coming. He could feel his spunk already surging in his cock, like the effervescing fluid in some test-tube. He had to do something, to think of something to prevent the worst, most humiliating fiasco of his life. He had to damp it down, push it back down. What would serve as an instant bromide, a circuit-breaker for this electric spasm? Not his old girlfriend's homey, suety body – that was an erotic image, if not as erotic as what now lay beneath him panting, urging him on. Not his father's face creased with sincerity – although that helped some. No, it had to be something definitively unerotic, something that would transcendentally turn him off . . .

'Fuck me!' Ursula exhorted him. Her heels were against his buttocks, she was urging him on. 'Fuck me!' she squealed into the nape of his neck. Her nails tore at his exposed shoulders. Then the solution came to him, and with it the correct, crucial damper. Bell! He would think of Bell. Bell's white, domed forehead; Bell's damp, lubricious mouth; Bell's black, black hair. He would use Bell to turn himself off, to avert disaster.

And with this settled, Richard was able once more to rear upward over the prone form of Ursula, to plunge into her with renewed vigour, adamantine confidence.

Her mouth lolled open. Her eyes rolled back in ecstasis. Her hair lay in a fan about her head. Her features were transfigured . . . No, not transfigured, *transforming*! They were changing, being replaced by other, stronger, more brutish features. Ursula's forehead was bulging, growing whiter, she was being instantly encephalicised. And the arms that held Richard, they

too were changing, becoming thicker, more muscular, hairier. He tried to pull away, but the legs that grasped him above the hips were thicker now as well. Horribly thick and imprisoning. As Richard watched in awed fascination, the beautiful breasts he had been licking and sucking withered, expanded into hard dinner plates of pectoral, each pap sporting a twistle of black, black hair.

Richard's cock died. It didn't slither out of its soft confinement – it was spat out. It wasn't Ursula's voice that was urging Richard on any more, it was a deeper, throatier voice, a voice not of abandonment – but of damnation.

Bell hugged Richard to his great chest. He stroked Richard's blond curls and cupped his cheek with a blunt hand. Richard couldn't understand why it was that he could hear what Bell was saying, because his own screams bounced and whined around the room. 'It's good to have you on board,' said the big man; 'I thought you were never really going to join – become one of us.'

And as he pulled Richard down on top of him, the scent of Jicki came into the back of Richard's throat. But it was no longer sweet, it was bitter, bitter as cocaine.

A NOTE ABOUT THE AUTHOR
AND ILLUSTRATOR

Will Self is the author of many novels and books of non-fiction, including *How the Dead Live*, which was shortlisted for the Whitbread Novel of the Year 2002, *The Butt*, winner of the Bollinger Everyman Wodehouse Prize for Comic Fiction 2008, and, with Ralph Steadman, *Psychogeography* and *Psycho Too*. He lives in South London.

Martin Rowson is one of Britain's leading politica cartoonists and has produced comic book versions of T. S. Eliot's *The Waste Land* and Lawrence Sterne's *Tristram Shandy*.